W9-BGK-680

This book belongs to

....

....

GROSSET & DUNLAP
Published by the Penguin Group
Penguin Group (USA) LLC, 375 Hudson Street, New York, New York 10014, USA

USA | Canada | UK | Ireland | Australia | New Zealand | India | South Africa | China
penguin.com
A Penguin Random House Company

Penguin supports copyright. Copyright fuels creativity, encourages diverse voices, promotes free speech,
and creates a vibrant culture. Thank you for buying an authorized edition of this book and for complying with copyright laws
by not reproducing, scanning, or distributing any part of it in any form without permission.
You are supporting writers and allowing Penguin to continue to publish books for every reader.

Copyright © 2004 by Eric Hill. All rights reserved. Published in 2005 by Grosset & Dunlap,
a division of Penguin Young Readers Group, 345 Hudson Street, New York, New York 10014.
GROSSET & DUNLAP is a trademark of Penguin Group (USA) LLC.
Original edition first published in Great Britain 2004 by Frederick Warne & Co. Planned and produced by Ventura Publishing
Ltd. 80 Strand, London WC2R 0RL, England. Manufactured in China.

ISBN 978-0-448-48837-0 • July 2014

2 4 6 8 10 9 7 5 3 1

Night-Night, Spot

Eric Hill

Grosset & Dunlap • New York

It was getting late. Spot had finished his supper. Now he was busy playing with his train, his blocks, and his ball.

Sally looked in.
"Time for bed, Spot," she said.
"But, Mom," said Spot,
"I'm not sleepy!"

"You can put away your toys," said Sally.
"That will help to make you sleepy."
"All right, Mom," said Spot.

He put away his train, his blocks, and
his ball. "I'm still not sleepy!" said Spot.

"A nice warm bath will help," said Sam, Spot's dad. He filled the bath with lovely warm bubbles for Spot. Spot stayed in the bath for a long time, playing with his boat and his duck.

But when it was time to come out,
Spot still wasn't sleepy–not even
when Sam wrapped him in a big,
fluffy towel!

"I'll read you a story," said Sally. "That will send you off to sleep."

Sally read Spot his favorite story. It was all about pirates and their adventures on the high seas.

"Read it again, please," said Spot, when she had finished.

So Sally read the story again. "Thanks, Mom," said Spot. "Maybe I can go to sleep now."

"Just close your eyes and you'll soon drift into dreamland," said Sally. Spot closed his eyes and Sally kissed him goodnight. Then she tiptoed out of the room.

But Spot STILL wasn't sleepy!

"I can't stay in bed when I'm not sleepy," he said to himself.

"I'll get up and pretend to be a pirate, like the ones in my storybook."

Spot went to his toy chest. He got out an eye
patch, a bandana, and a wooden sword.

"Yo-ho-ho!" he said,
jumping up and down.
"I'm the pirate king
of the high seas!"

After a while, Spot got tired of being a pirate.
But he still wasn't sleepy!

"I'll pretend to be something else now," he said,
looking in his toy chest.

"What will I be?"

"I'll be a cowboy!" Spot decided.

He put on his cowboy hat and he found his horse.
Spot rode his horse all around the room.
Stomp! Stomp! Stomp!

"I'm a buckaroo!" he shouted. "This is so much fun–it's a good thing I'm not sleepy!"

Sally came to the door. "You're supposed to be asleep!" she called. "What's all the noise about?"

But Spot didn't answer.

That's because Spot didn't hear her. He was curled up in his cowboy costume—fast asleep!

Sally picked up Spot, took off his costume, and tucked him into bed.

"I think I was sleepy after all, Mom," he murmured.

"I think you were," said Sally, smiling. She gave Spot a hug and another goodnight kiss.

"Sweet dreams, Spot! Night-night!"